Agatha Parrot
AND THE Thirteenth Chicken

Agatha Parrot

AND THE Thirteenth Chicken

TYPED OUT NEATLY BY
KJARTAN POSKITT

ILLUSTRATED BY
WES HARGIS

CLARION BOOKS

HOUGHTON MIFFLIN HARCOURT

BOSTON NEW YORK

Clarion Books
3 Park Avenue
New York, New York 10016

Clarion Books is an imprint of Houghton Mifflin Harcourt Publishing Company.

www.hmhco.com

The text was set in Adobe Caslon Pro.

Design by Lisa Vega

Library of Congress Cataloging-in-Publication Data
Names: Poskitt, Kjartan, author. | Hargis, Wes, illustrator.
Title: Agatha Parrot and the thirteenth chicken / typed out neatly by Kjartan Poskitt ; illustrated by Wes Hargis.
Description: Boston ; New York : Clarion Books, Houghton Mifflin Harcourt, [2017] | Originally published in the United Kingdom by Egmont in 2013. | Summary: "Agatha Parrot and her friends babysit a flock of newly-hatched chicks for a back-to-school project"— Provided by publisher.
Identifiers: LCCN 2016016156 | ISBN 9780544509092 (hardback)
Subjects: | CYAC: Chickens—Fiction. | Animals—Infancy—Fiction. | Schools—Fiction. | Humorous stories. | BISAC: JUVENILE FICTION / School & Education. | JUVENILE FICTION / Humorous Stories. | JUVENILE FICTION / Girls & Women. | JUVENILE FICTION / Social Issues / Friendship. | JUVENILE FICTION / Animals / Birds. | JUVENILE FICTION / Mysteries & Detective Stories.
Classification: LCC PZ7.1.P65 Ai 2017 | DDC [Fic]—dc23
LC record available at https://lccn.loc.gov/2016016156

Manufactured in the United States of America
DOC 10 9 8 7 6 5 4 3 2 1
4500656979

This book is dedicated to

Gilbert,

for making Ivy's mom

SO happy. xxx

No chickens were hurt
during the course of
writing this book, because
chickens are good and
we LIKE chickens.

THE GANG!

Agatha (that's me). One time I had my hair combed for a photo and nobody knew who I was. And that's true.
Ivy refuses to eat cabbage, but she can put spiders in her mouth!
Martha says she never looks for old potato chips between the couch cushions, but she does.

Contents

The Little New Things

Hiya!

I hope you like books written by somebody who once tipped a whole box of cornflakes over her head. That's me!

Don't worry—I'm not completely crazy. I had a very good reason for the cornflake thing: I thought a giant ghost chicken had burst out of a lump in the wallpaper. If you were me you'd have done exactly the same thing, honest! You'll understand why when you've read the story, so let's start at the beginning.

My name is Agatha Jane Parrot, and I go to Odd Street School, which is at the end of Odd Street, where I live. And even though the cornflake thing makes perfect sense, there's one thing about me that I have to admit is pretty embarrassing.

I just LOVE the first day back at school after vacation.

I know that's weird. School is full of lessons, rules, being quiet, tests, old lady teachers, multiplication tables, and freezing cold bathrooms—shiver shiver YUCK!

But the reason I can't wait to get back is that there's always a NEW THING.

Sometimes it's really obvious, like when they

built a jungle gym with a slide on the playground! It was just so awesome. EVERYBODY slid on it including our new teacher, Miss Pingle, even though she says she didn't. Miss Pingle is super cool because her hair changes color every week, and we ALL saw her taking a quick turn on the slide when she thought nobody was watching. She didn't know we were looking out the library window. She came sliding down, waving her hands in the air, and went WHEEEE really loud, and we heard her— ha ha!

But the last time we got back to school after a break, there wasn't a big new thing like the jungle gym, so me and my friends went around looking for little new things. Here's what the others found, and I can tell you that one of them is very important in the story later on! See if you can guess which one it is.

1) Bianca Bayuss noticed that the rubber plant in our class had grown a new leaf. Oooh . . . Could this be important in the story? Maybe the plant grows more and more leaves and turns the whole school into a jungle with tigers and elephants? Actually, it doesn't, but it would be neat if it did.

2) Martha Swan saw that Miss Pingle had a new bag exactly the same color as her hair. How cool is that? We had a big argument about what color

Miss P.'s bag/hair was. I said purple, but Martha said dark red, and Bianca said it was maroon. So we asked Miss P. The answer was *Damson Dream*—we'd never have guessed that in a million years.

3) Ivy Malting spotted that Miss Wizzit had gotten her ears pierced! Miss Wizzit is the school receptionist, and her main job is guarding the photocopier. She HATES when anybody uses it, and there's no way she would have left it while she snuck off to get her ears done. Ivy says that Miss Wizzit probably pierced her ears herself with the stapler. Ugh! Sorry, you'll have to block that thought out. Think about daisies and doughnuts and happy things. La-la la-la lah . . .

4) Ellie Slippin said Motley the custodian had

grown a green mustache! It turns out he'd had a mug of pea soup and some of it had gotten stuck to his top lip. It's not surprising that it fooled us, though, because it was there for three days, until our principal, Mrs. Twelvetrees, told him about it.

So which new thing do you think comes into the story? Is it the rubber plant, the bag, Miss Wizzit's ears, or the green mustache? And what new thing did I find?

If you want to know, keep reading!

The Big New Thing

I didn't find my new thing until the Monday after we got back. I was going past the reception desk when the door buzzer rang. Miss Wizzit pushed a button and spoke into the intercom.

"Wizzit?" asked Miss Wizzit.

"Greetings," said a voice. "We are the Eggs Experience company."

"Kitchen deliveries go to the kitchen door," snapped Miss Wizzit.

"It's not for the kitchen," said the voice. "The children are going to hatch the eggs."

Miss Wizzit made the sort of face that you can only make if you're Miss Wizzit imagining lots of kids sitting on nests full of eggs.

"Don't be silly," said Miss Wizzit, but then Mrs. Twelvetrees came dashing out of her office.

"Is that the egg people?" she gushed, all excited. "Let them in, Miss Wizzit."

Egg people? WOW! What an exciting new thing. It was even better than Motley's green mustache.

The egg people were two men with bushy beards, and they were wearing long hairy robes and sandals. One of them had an old basket covered with a red towel, and the other one had a big plastic box with a wire coming out of it.

"Here are the fruits of our feathered community," said the one with the basket. He pulled the towel away to reveal a bunch of eggs sitting on some straw.

"And here is the electric mother," said the other one.

"The what?" asked Miss Wizzit.

"It's the incubator to make the eggs hatch," said Mrs. Twelvetrees.

The egg people put the eggs and the incubator on the desk, and one of them passed an envelope to Mrs. Twelvetrees.

"We leave you in peace," said the egg people, then they both bowed polite little bows and left.

"Aren't the egg people just wonderful?" said

Mrs. T. "They live in a cave and grow their own clothes. It's a mystery how they survive!"

"What izzit?" asked Miss Wizzit, pointing at the envelope.

Mrs. Twelvetrees looked inside.

"It's a bill for five hundred dollars," she said.

"Mystery solved," said Miss Wizzit.

Chicken Crazy

It was going to take a day or two for the eggs to hatch, so the incubator was set up in the little kiddies' class, where old Miss Bunn teaches. You wouldn't think there would be much excitement about a plastic box full of eggs sitting on a table doing nothing, would you?

WRONG!

All the kiddies went chicken crazy.

To start with, Miss Bunn gathered them around the plinky-plonk piano and taught them one of the greatest songs in the world. You must know it—it goes:

Chick chick chick chick

CHICKEN!

Lay a little egg for me.

Chick chick chick chick

CHICKEN!

Lay one, lay two, lay three!

(Did you sing that out loud when you read it? If you did, then you are a STAR! Have a round of applause—clap clap clap.)

The next day, Miss Bunn had all the kiddies make chicken hats out of yellow paper, completing them with orange cardboard beaks. Of course none of the kiddies could wait for the glue to dry, so they all put the hats on, and the hats got stuck to their hair. AWESOME!

But that wasn't the best part. The BEST part was the giant chicken picture they drew to cover their classroom door. It was supposed to be one big chicken, but all the kiddies had taken turns drawing on the wings and legs and other parts. It

ended up with seven feet, thirty tiny wings, five beaks (most of them with teeth), three hands, sunglasses, a pirate flag, and a flower growing out of its tail.

Recess was crazy. We were all outside surrounded by chicken-headed little kiddies who were running around and screaming, "Chick chick chick chick CHICKEN!"

It was all completely fabulous except for one thing, and that one thing was called Gwendoline Tutt. Gwendoline is in a different class from us, **THANK GOODNESS.** She's the scrawny one with the pink bike who lives in the biggest house on Odd Street, and she's far too snotty for anything.

"Give it a rest!" shouted Gwendoline. "Honestly! A few eggs and the whole school gets stupid."

We all knew why Gwendoline was in a mood. Gwendoline had wanted the eggs to be in her class, and Gwendoline

doesn't like it when Gwendoline doesn't get what Gwendoline wants. But if she thought she could spoil the fun, she was wrong. Miss Bunn came to the door and called the kiddies over.

"One of the eggs is moving," said Miss Bunn.

"Oooooh!" said the kiddies.

"That means the first chicken is getting ready to come out!" said Miss Bunn.

The kiddies all shouted, "CHICK CHICK CHICK CHICK CHICKEN!"

After recess, me and Martha went to Miss Bunn's classroom and looked in the door. All the kiddies were around the table, and Miss Bunn had taken the lid off the incubator.

"Let's see if any chickens can hear me," said Miss

Bunn. She clicked her tongue a few times, then said to the eggs, "Hello, little chickens!"

Everyone listened carefully. Sure enough, a small squeaky noise came from one of the eggs! Me and Martha even heard it from over by the door.

"That is so cool!" said Martha.

"Would anybody else like to say hello?" asked Miss Bunn.

Immediately every single kiddie started screaming at the egg. "CHICK CHICK CHICK CHICK CHICKEN!"

The egg got very quiet. I don't blame it. I bet the chicken changed its mind about hatching and decided to stay inside. Imagine being born and the first thing you see are all these giant kiddies with orange beaks growing out of their heads, screaming at you. Scary!

The next morning was Wednesday, and as soon as Motley opened the school doors, all the kiddies charged in, still wearing their chicken hats. WOO-HOO! They ran down the corridor tossing their coats and lunch bags everywhere, then burst into their classroom to see what had happened.

Miss Bunn was staring at a few yellow blobs in the incubator.

"We've got four so far," said Miss Bunn.

"OOOOOH!" said the kiddies.

Nobody in school could concentrate for the whole day. Every so often a huge shout of "Chick chick chick chick CHICKEN!" would echo from

Miss Bunn's class as another chicken appeared. By recess there were seven chicks, by lunchtime there were eleven, and by afternoon the last two eggs had hatched, which made thirteen chickens altogether.

All the other classes took turns going to see the chicks in the incubator. When we went in, Miss Bunn was clearing some pieces of shell away. The chicks looked a little wet from being inside the eggs.

"They need to stay in the incubator tonight," said Miss Bunn. "By tomorrow they'll be dried out and fluffy, and then they'll need somewhere bigger to live."

It all sounded so simple, didn't it?

It wasn't!

Motley's Box of Great Mystery

On Thursday we were all in class when the door burst open and Motley came in walking backwards. He was carrying one end of an old recycling box, and big Mrs. Potts the lunchroom lady was carrying the other end. The box had some old chair legs sticking out of the top of it, and dangling between them was a shiny metal lampshade that was banging into everything. Motley and big Mrs. Potts managed to squeeze their way past our chairs without killing anybody, and then they plunked the whole thing down on the table by the window.

Motley straightened it up and gave it a wipe with his cloth, then stood back and grinned at us proudly.

"It's very nice," said Miss Pingle, trying to be polite.

"Yes, it's very nice," we all said, and then we were all quiet.

Poor old Motley. I think he'd expected us to give him a round of applause. He looked a little sad.

"All right, then," he said. "There it is. We'll leave you to it."

Big Mrs. Potts obviously felt sorry for him. "I thought they'd be pleased," she said.

"Me too," said Motley.

They were shuffling their way back to the door when Ivy blurted out, "What is it?"

"It's a brooding box for the chickens, of course," said Motley. "It's too big to fit in Miss Bunn's classroom, so the chickens will have to come in here."

"WAHOO!" we all cheered, and Motley beamed.

"Mr. Motley has fixed up this heating lamp," explained big Mrs. Potts. "It used to hang in my kitchen to keep the food warm."

"But what if the lamp makes the chickens too hot?" asked Miss Pingle.

"Mr. Motley thought of that," said big Mrs. Potts. "Didn't you, Mr. Motley?"

"Of course," said Motley. "That's the clever part of my invention."

He pointed at the side of the box. There was a switch, and next to it was a control knob with numbers around it.

"If you want to make it hotter or colder, you turn this knob," he said.

"He's so clever," said big Mrs. Potts.

Then big Mrs. Potts took Motley off to have a cup of coffee, I think, but I don't know for sure, because it's not like I followed them or anything.

The Potato-Headed Monster

As soon as we had Motley's box, we wanted to put the chickens in it, but we didn't dare go and get them from Miss Bunn's class while the kiddies were watching. There would have been a kiddie riot! That's not funny, either—my sister, Tilly, is in that class, and she says that some of her sweet little friends BITE. Eeek!

We had to wait until after school, when all the

kiddies had gone home. In the end, the only people left were me, Ellie, Martha, Bianca, Ivy, and Miss Pingle, but at least we'd had time to get Motley's box ready.

There was a great big bag of chicken food, and Martha loves food, so she took charge of it. If she'd been a chicken she'd have eaten all of it at once, so she wasn't too impressed when she was only allowed to put a little bit onto a tiny plastic saucer.

"That's not enough for thirteen chickens!" said Martha. "I'll go home and get a cereal bowl."

"No!" said Miss Pingle.

Ivy filled up a little water bowl, and me and Ellie put some paper towels on the bottom of the box, because that's what little chicks like to walk on.*

(*Interesting fact! Chickens don't like to walk

on newspaper because it's too slippery for their feet, and they can get dirty from the ink, too. And newspapers are covered in words, but little chickens can't read, so it's unfair to them. And that's true.)

Miss Pingle had gotten some wood shavings to put in the box so the chickens could snuggle up and keep warm, and Bianca made a big sign with a picture of a chicken on it. Bianca makes really good

pictures, but I wanted her to draw a flower growing out of its tail just like the one on the kiddies' picture! I was dying to ask her to, but I thought she might get annoyed, so I didn't.

Everything was ready when Mrs. Twelvetrees came in carrying the incubator. Inside were the little chickens.

HOORAY!

Mrs. T. went over to the table by the window and saw Bianca's sign.

"What a lovely picture," said Mrs. T. "But isn't it supposed to have a flower growing out of its tail?"

"HA HA HA!" Bianca laughed.

Bah! I wished I'd asked.

Mrs. Twelvetrees checked inside the box.

"Well done, girls!" she said. "I see you've put

some paper towels down to keep them from sliding around."

"And to catch all the poop," said Ivy.

"Er, yes," said Mrs. T. "That too."

Mrs. T. took the lid off the incubator. "They've gotten quite warm in here, so let them run around a little before you put them into Mr. Motley's box."

Mrs. Twelvetrees put the incubator on the floor and tipped it up a bit. WHEEE!

The chickens all rolled out, then they got on their feet and started toddling around.

Awww . . . CUTE!

"The whole school is going to have a big chicken assembly tomorrow morning," said Mrs. T. "So don't be late!" Then off she went to do some other principal stuff.

The chickens were amazing, and we started naming them. There was Wizzy, who was really fast, and Tubby, who kept rolling over, and Bumper, who kept climbing on top of Moody Broody, who just sat there looking cross.

I couldn't pick a favorite because they were all my favorite, but if I had to pick a *favorite* favorite, it would be Random. That's because the others kept bunching up together, but Random was far too busy. He toddled off to admire the new leaf on the rubber plant, then he inspected the radiator pipes, and he finally ended up trying to peck a hole in Miss Pingle's bag.

It was all very happy until a voice came from the doorway.

"What is going on in HERE?"

Oh, rats. Miss Barking had come in. She's the vice principal, who has big square glasses and thinks that everything in the world is  dangerous. One time she tried to shut the whole school down because she saw a furry slug under the radiator in the library, but we all knew it was just an old piece of candy. Of course we didn't tell her that—we just watched her freak out when Martha wiped the dust off and popped the candy into her mouth. HA HA awesome!

Standing behind Miss Barking was Gwendoline Tutt.

"Look, Miss Barking," said Gwendoline in her horrible snotty voice. "Those chickens are all over the floor. I don't think that's very hygienic, do you, Miss Barking?"

Honestly! If anything isn't hygienic, it's Gwendoline. She always makes us feel sick. She must have been spying on us and then gone to fetch Miss Barking.

"Those chickens could be carrying a nasty disease," said Miss Barking.

We were about to protest, but then Random decided that Gwendoline's shoes were really interesting. He hurried over to have a good look.

Toddle toddle toddle—poop!

WAHOO! Random had done a little you-know-what right in front of Gwendoline! It was only the tiniest little blob that had splotted onto the floor, but Gwendoline made the most of it.

"Urgh, that's totally GROSS!" she shouted, then ran out the door.

What a baby! But Miss Barking wasn't taking any chances.

"Keep back, children," said Miss B., staring at the blob like it was radioactive. "There could be dangerous fumes filling the room."

Huh.

She made us all line up against the far wall, and opened the window. Then she reached into her bag and got out one of those paper facemasks that go over your mouth and nose. When she put it on, her head looked like a giant potato wearing glasses.

"Do you have safety gloves, Miss Pingle?" asked the giant potato.

Miss Pingle shook her head.

"Really, Miss Pingle," said the potato. "Those little beaks are like needles and could inject you with chicken germs. Luckily for you, I have come prepared."

Miss Barking pulled on a massive pair of gloves that made her hands look three times bigger. She got some wipes out of her bag to clear the little blob up, then went crawling across the floor to catch the tiny little chickens. Poor things! Can you imagine being one day old and being chased by a giant potato with monster hands? Not nice.

Eventually she got all the chicks into Motley's box.

"We need to turn the heat lamp on," said Miss Pingle.

Miss Pingle was about to push the switch when Miss Barking stopped her.

"GLOVES!" said Miss B. strictly. "How do you know this electrical device is completely safe? Has it been tested? Does it have a certificate?"

Miss P. sighed and let Miss Barking take over. Miss B. turned the switch, but the light didn't come on.

"Just as I thought," she said. "It's broken."

"Maybe you have to adjust the temperature with the knob," suggested Miss P.

Miss Barking grabbed the knob in her big glove and turned it all the way up. The light came on.

"There," she said.

"That looks too hot," said Miss P. "Can you turn it down a bit?"

Miss Barking grabbed the knob again and turned it back. The light went off.

"That's a little too far," said Miss Pingle.

"I KNOW what I'm doing, thank you, Miss Pingle!" said Miss Barking sharply. Then she gave the knob one more turn.

"There . . . oh!"

Her giant hand had broken off the control knob! The light over the box was blazing full blast.

"Yeep yeep yeep!" went the chickens.

"Oh, no!" said Ivy. "Miss Barking is cooking the baby chickens!"

Miss Barking tried to push the knob back into place, but it kept falling off.

Eeek! I couldn't watch anymore, so I ran off to get Motley. As soon as he came in and saw the light on full blast, he unplugged the box from the wall. Off it went—*phew!*

Motley saw the broken knob lying on the table. "Who did this?" he said crossly.

"I must go home," said Miss Barking suddenly, and she dashed out the door, still wearing her mask and gloves.

"Yeah, fly back to your own planet," muttered Motley as she went. (Oooh! That was a mean thing to say, but she *had* broken his box, so we didn't really blame him.) Motley picked up the broken knob. "It'll take me all night to fix it."

"If the chickens don't have a heater, they'll get cold," said Miss Pingle.

"We'll look after them," I said. "They can come and stay at our houses!"

Miss Pingle thought about it. "As long as you keep them warm, they should be all right for one night," she said. "Just make sure they get plenty of water to drink."

"And plenty of food," said Martha, picking up the food bag.

Eeek! I suddenly had this vision of Martha shoving the whole bag inside one little chicken, and judging by Miss Pingle's face, she was having the same vision!

"Put that down!" said Miss Pingle. "That stays here."

"So what can they eat?" demanded Martha.

"They can have Gilbert's food," said Ivy. "We've got lots of it."

"Who's Gilbert?" asked Miss Pingle.

"Mom's goldfish," said Ivy. "But he's nearly dead, so he doesn't need it."

"NO!" said Miss Pingle firmly. "The chickens will not need to be fed for one night. But we do need something to keep them in."

"There's a bunch of shoeboxes in Miss Bunn's classroom," I said. "We could use them to take the chickens home."

"Not me!" Ellie whimpered. "I don't dare to! I had a bad dream about chickens."

"Chickens aren't scary!" we said.

"They are when they've got poisonous beaks and peck through your tights," said Ellie. "My leg fell off in my dream."

So I went to get four shoeboxes, one each for me, Martha, Ivy, and Bianca, but not one for Ellie in case a chicken pecked through her tights and made her leg fall off.

"Thank you," said Miss Pingle. "I'll pack up the chickens and bring them down to the playground. You get your coats, and then ask your mothers if you can take the chickens home."

So we all ran out to the playground and asked our moms. Martha's mom got the wrong idea. "You want to bring some chickens home?" she said. "But I've already got dinner planned. It's pork chops and veggies."

"We're not eating the chickens, Mom!" explained Martha. "We're looking after them. Maybe we could give them some pork chops and veggies for their dinner."

"NO!" we all said.

Miss Pingle turned up with the four shoeboxes and gave us one each, except for Ellie.

"I've taped the lids down, so don't open them until you get home," said Miss P. "And tonight, make sure they have a little bowl of water, and keep them warm. I want to see them all back here tomorrow!"

Who's in the Box?

I made Mom and Tilly walk home really fast because I couldn't wait to see who was in my box! Since there were thirteen chickens, we should have gotten three chicks each, but one lucky person would get an extra chicken. I was hoping I'd be the lucky one, and I REALLY hoped the extra chick was Random! Anybody who toddles up to

Gwendoline and poops right in front of her is my hero for life. He was so cool.

When we opened the front door, we saw lots of old towels by the stairs. Dad was halfway up the staircase, trying to balance the stepladder on a kitchen chair. It looked lethal.

"Keep back!" said Dad. "I'm decorating."

"Do you have to do that now?" asked Mom.

"You're the one who wanted new wallpaper," said Dad.

Mom just told me to take the chickens upstairs out of the way.

I squeezed past the stepladder with Tilly following me. We went into our bedroom, and I put the box on the chair. I was just about to open it . . . BIG EXCITEMENT! . . . but then Dad shouted:

"Agatha! Quick, I need you!"

I went out and saw he'd taken his shoes off and was balancing on the banister. He was holding a tape measure up to the ceiling, and I had to hold it

at the bottom of the wall so he could see how high the ceiling was.

I was only gone for about five seconds, but if you've got a nosy interfering little sister, you'll know what's coming next.

When I got back, the box was upside down on the floor and Tilly's legs were sticking out from under our bunk beds. OOOOH, I WAS SO MAD! Obviously she'd opened the box and dropped it, and the chickens had run off to hide.

I crawled under the bunks and saw an old blue sock hopping up and down. I managed to grab it and found that one of the chicks had gotten his head stuck inside it. Tilly spotted another chick right in the corner behind the leg of the bunk beds, pecking at a dust bunny. I snagged both chicks and put

them back in the box. Then I went to take another look.

There was no sign of any more, so we had to pull everything out from under the bed. I found my horrible old woolly tights, which I'd stuffed down there years ago to lose on purpose (yuck!). Plus there were my lost earphones (hooray!), pencils, old birthday cards, bags, a gym shoe, some Lego bricks, tons of hairy fluff, dead spiders, a not-quite-dead spider (EEEK!!!), and seventeen cents.

"How many chickens were there in the box?" I asked Tilly.

"They ran away," said Tilly.

Fat lot of help that was!

Just then there was a grumpy noise from outside the door.

"What's the matter, Dad?" I asked.

"I just stepped on something squishy."

I dashed out to see him sitting on the carpet pulling off his sock. There was a yellow blob stuck on it.

"Oh, no!" I said. "It's one of our chickens!"

"A *chicken?*" said Dad.

He sniffed it.

"No, it's a piece of cake," said Dad. "What's a piece of cake doing up here? JAMES?"

At that point my brother, James, stuck his head out of his room.

"James, have you been bringing food upstairs?"

"Ummm," said James, shaking his head, but it was obvious his mouth was full, plus he had crumbs stuck to his sweater. In fact, there was a trail of crumbs leading along the landing, and there at the end was a little yellow thing happily helping himself to a cake feast.

"It's Tubby!" I said.

At last we had three chickens safely back in the

box. One of them was definitely Tubby, but none of them was Random. Never mind.

Whoever they were, we were going to have an AWESOME time!

Chicken Soccer

After dinner, I thought my chickens needed some friends to play with, so I went next door to Martha's house.

I rang the bell, but nothing happened. Maybe Martha was still having dinner? Then I had a nasty thought. I hoped she wasn't trying to feed her chickens pork chops and veggies!

Suddenly there was a big *POP* sound from inside, and then Martha opened the door.

"What was that noise?" I said.

"Just a balloon!" Martha laughed.

"Are you sure?" I said.

"Of course I'm sure," said Martha. "I was practicing soccer moves with it, and it burst."

"Thank goodness," I said. "I thought you'd been feeding your chickens pork chops and veggies and one of them had exploded."

"Don't you trust me?" said Martha. She stomped off to get her shoebox. Inside were three little chickens.

"Happy now?" she said.

I felt bad for doubting Martha and for upsetting

her too, but I had the perfect idea for how to make it up to her.

"How about if my chickens challenge your chickens to a soccer game?"

"Cool!" Martha grinned.

Martha brought her shoebox to my house, and we made a soccer field on the kitchen table, with little Lego goalposts. It was perfect because our table is near the radiator, so the chickens wouldn't get too cold. Martha put her chickens at one end, and I put mine at the other end, and we put an old Ping-Pong ball in the middle.

It was really funny! The chickens toddled over and knocked the ball around. I suppose it should have been Martha's team against my team, playing three against three, but it was more like every chicken for itself. If real soccer was like that and had a ball as big as the people, it would be a lot more interesting!

There was just one thing missing from the game. We didn't have Random! Where was that star quality? Where was the creative play in midfield? Who was there to create chances and open up the defense? (No, I don't know what any of that means either, but it's what they say on TV.) Actually, Tubby did show a bit of star quality when he tried to eat one of the goalposts—ha ha!

"We need more players," said Martha.

"I'll get Ivy," I said.

I left Martha and went to knock on Ivy's door, but then I looked up. Ivy was sitting by her bedroom window with her chickens running about on the windowsill.

"It's AGATHA!" shouted Ivy to the chickens. "Everybody wave at Agatha!"

Ivy held up one of her chickens, and so I waved at it. Ivy waved back, but being a bit crazy, she can't just wave a little wave. She waved a giant big wave still holding the chicken.

"CAREFUL!" I shouted.

Ivy disappeared from the window. Then I heard her come downstairs, four steps at a time (as usual).

WAM BAM BAM WUMP!

Ivy's door opened, and there she was with her shoebox.

"We're having a chicken soccer game," I said.

"Awesome!" said Ivy.

"How many do you have?"

"Three," said Ivy.

"Are you sure?" I asked her. "What about the one you were waving?"

"You mean Mr. Thompson?" asked Ivy. "He's back in the box."

"Can I see?" I said. I felt I had to check.

It's not that I don't trust Ivy—it's just that Ivy can be a little nutty.

Ivy opened her box. Sure enough, she had three chickens.

"There's Mr. Thompson," she said. "And that's Lovely, and that's Drain Pump."

Ha ha! I didn't expect Ivy to give her chickens normal names, but where did she get Drain Pump from?

"It's in the book I'm reading," said Ivy.

"What book?"

"*Washing Machine Instructions*," said Ivy. "I've only got four more pages to go."

You see what I mean about Ivy?

Soon we had nine chickens running around on

the kitchen table. It wasn't hard to tell who they all were. I had Tubby, and my other two were Bib and Bob. Martha had brought Wizzy and Bumper and one she called Peckham, who had an extra little funny tuft of fluff. Ivy's chickens were all huddled together like a ball with six legs, but there was still no sign of Random.

"Bianca must have the other four chicks," I said. "Let's see if she wants to bring hers over too."

So Martha went to Bianca's house and came back with her shoebox.

"Is Bianca coming?" I asked.

"No, she's got to practice her trombone," said Martha. "But she said we can borrow her chickens."

We opened up Bianca's box . . . OH, DEAR!

We had expected to see four chicks, but there were only three. Right away, I knew which one was missing!

Where was Random?

I was worried sick. When Tilly had let the chicks escape from my box, I thought I'd caught them all. Maybe I hadn't. Maybe Random was still running around somewhere!

I had to try to keep cool so that Martha and Ivy didn't know I was panicking. I decided to double-check their stories.

"So, Martha," I said. "Are you sure you didn't feed your chickens anything? Not even one sliver of pork and a tiny bit of cabbage?"

"And one drop of gravy?" asked Ivy, getting into the spirit of things.

"Why?" asked Martha.

"I just thought that maybe one of your chickens exploded and you'd forgotten?"

"NO WAY!" snapped Martha.

I hadn't meant to offend Martha, and I quickly turned to Ivy.

"So, Ivy," I said. "You've got three chickens now, but think carefully. When you opened the box, was it a different number?"

"Like what?" said Ivy.

"Like *four*, perhaps?" I said. "It's just that I saw you waving Mr. Thompson around . . ."

"Are you're suggesting I might have accidentally thrown a chicken away?" asked Ivy.

"I didn't say that . . ."

"But you MEANT it."

Now I'd offended Ivy, too. I had opened my mouth to apologize when the doorbell rang. It was Ivy's mom, and she looked very sad.

"Can Ivy come home?" she asked. "Just for a minute?"

"What's up?" said Ivy.

"I need you," said Ivy's mom. Then she started to sniff and wipe her eyes, so Ivy went to see what the matter was.

What's Tocking the Bloob Up?

After Ivy had gone, me and Martha put the chickens back into their boxes. It was awful, because we were both counting them over and over, but it didn't make any difference. There were only twelve, and there should have been thirteen.

"It wasn't me who lost a chicken," said Martha. "Maybe it was you?"

"No no, not me, impossible," I said. I was trying

to act casual, but my voice went all squeaky, and I knew my face was red.

Then Dad came into the kitchen to get a bucket of water.

"Be careful on the stairs Agatha," said Dad. "It's a little sticky, so don't let those chickens go running around up there again. Remember, I nearly stepped on one."

He left. Martha was staring at me, furious.

"You were trying to blame me and Ivy!" she snapped. "And all the time I bet it's your fault."

"No, no, no!" I said. "Maybe Bianca knows what happened. Let's go and ask her."

"We can't ask her now," said Martha. "She's playing her trombone. Listen—you'll hear it."

So we listened, but the funny thing was that we *didn't* hear it!

Normally when Bianca plays her trombone, everybody on Odd Street can hear her going *bwarb bab barp*. One time she was learning a new note called BOTTOM B FLAT, which made all the glasses rattle in our cabinet! My brother, James, does a few BOTTOM B FLAT noises sometimes too, and he doesn't even have a trombone. Typical boy.

Martha and me went outside, but we still couldn't hear anything, even though Bianca's bedroom window was open. We saw her moving around inside.

"Hey, Bianca!" shouted Martha. "We thought you were playing your trombone."

"I'm trying," said Bianca. "But something is tocking the bloob up."

Tocking the bloob up? We love Bianca, but sometimes we have to work out what she's saying. She tried again.

"It's bloobing the tock up."

It was no use. So instead of trying to explain any more, Bianca stuck her trombone out the window and gave it a mighty blow. Her cheeks swelled up like she was swallowing two apples at once, but no sound came out.

"I know what she means!" I said.

"Me too!" said Martha.

"Something is blocking the tube up!" we both said.

Then suddenly . . .

PLOP . . . BWARBBBB . . . *wheeeee!*

A fluffy yellow lump shot out of the end of the trombone along with a massive blast of BOTTOM B FLAT. The lump flew over our heads, and normally Odd Street is really empty because it's a dead end, but just then Gwendoline Tutt went by on her pink bike, and the yellow lump landed on her shoulder.

"Did you see that?" gasped Martha.

"It was Random!" I said. "He must have gotten out of Bianca's box and climbed into her trombone."

By this time Gwendoline was farther up the street—all the way past number 13—and me and Martha were running after her.

"Gwendoline!" we shouted. "COME BACK!"

"Can't catch me, losers!" said Gwendoline, and she pedaled faster.

Gwendolyn's house is number 59, and we had to run all the way there before she stopped. We were gasping for air.

"What do you two want?" Gwendoline demanded.

"Don't move," I said. "There's something on your shoulder. Let me get it."

But just as I was reaching out, Gwendoline noticed the yellow lump. She screamed and brushed it off onto the ground.

"UGH! What is it?" she shouted.

"It's a chicken," we said.

"It looks dead," said Gwendoline. "Serves it right."

OOOOOH, I WAS SO MAD! (Even madder than I was at Tilly on page 48.)

When Gwendoline opened the garage door to put her bike away, I could see all her dad's gardening stuff. Suddenly the lawn mower started itself and swallowed Gwendoline up, then gave a big burp. YIPPEE! Actually it didn't, but I promise you, if I was making this story up then I would definitely have put that in.

Meanwhile Martha had bent down to look at the yellow lump.

"I don't think it's the right color," said Martha. She picked it up carefully. Martha was right. I didn't know what it was, but at least I knew what it wasn't. It wasn't Random—thank goodness!

It was like a yellow fluffy sausage with a bit of string tied to the end. We took it back down the street and held it up so Bianca could see it.

"That's my trombone cleaner!" said Bianca. "I was looking for that."

"Gwendoline just tried to kill it," said Martha.

"She's weird," said Bianca.

Oh well. At least Random hadn't been blasted across the road by a BOTTOM B FLAT. But where was he?

A Sad Goodbye

When me and Martha got back to my house, Ellie came over to see the chickens. Typical Ellie: she loves numbers, so the first thing she did was count them.

"There's only twelve!" said Ellie.

"We know," I said. "It's really freaking us out."

"I'll tell you something even freakier," said Ellie. "Ivy was in her yard talking to a cactus in a pot."

"WHAT???"

Ivy lives next door at number 7, and the only place you can see her yard is from our bathroom window, so we all headed for the stairs.

Dad was on top of his wobbly ladder holding a long piece of soggy wallpaper.

"Where are you going?" he said.

"To the bathroom," I said.

"All of you?" said Dad. "Can't it wait?"

"No!" we said, and squeezed ourselves past the ladder.

"CAREFUL!" said Dad. Then he fell against the wall and got the paper stuck to his trousers, which was pretty funny, but we didn't stop to laugh. We had stuff to do.

Our bathroom window has fuzzy glass in it, and the only way you can see out is if you balance on the edge of the bathtub and open the window at the top. *Warning: Make sure the toilet lid is down.* One time Dad left the lid up when he climbed on the bathtub to change the light bulb. Then he slipped and his foot ended up in the toilet water—ha ha!

So there we were on the edge of the tub, looking down into Ivy's backyard. All we could see was a little cactus in a pot sitting on a kitchen chair and looking very important.

"See?" said Ellie. "I told you it was freaky."

Yes, it was a bit freaky, but it was nothing compared to some of the other things in Ivy's yard. For instance, it looks like there's a row of sticks growing out of the window box, but actually it's all the arms and legs that Ivy pulled off her Barbies.

We were still staring at the cactus when Ivy came out her back door. She was wearing an old black top hat, and she was carrying a piece of paper with writing on it. She walked around and around the little cactus very slowly, making low bell noises like this:

"Dong . . . dong . . . dong . . ."

Then she stood in front of the cactus and held

up the paper to read it. This is what she said:

"Go to sleep, my funny friend.

Rest your little head.

Your lovely dreams won't stop because you won't

  wake up.

You're dead.

It's sad we have to say goodbye,

And I don't want to spoil it.

That's why you're buried in a pot,

And not flushed down the toilet."

Then Ivy bent down, gave the cactus pot a little kiss, and went back indoors.

We were all very quiet.

Then all at once we went, "EEEK!"

The Magic Cactus

Me and Ellie and Martha were back in my kitchen, feeling a bit freaked out.

"Do you think Ivy had the extra chicken and buried it in the cactus pot?" asked Ellie.

"She told us she only had three," I said. "And Ivy doesn't lie."

It's true, she doesn't. Ivy might pull her dolls apart, and she might run up the down escalator at the mall, and she might pull her tights on over her head to pretend she's got legs growing out of her ears, but Ivy does not lie.

But we had to be sure, and we couldn't just say, "Did you kill Random and bury him in a pot?," could we?

"There's only one thing to do," I said. "We'll have to sneak into Ivy's yard and empty the pot to see what's in it."

"Ivy will know what we've done," said Martha. "My mom sells those cactuses in her shop, and if you tip one out, the dirt goes all over the place."

"That's right," said Ellie. "We got one last year, just like Ivy's. Same pot and everything."

Suddenly I was pulling at my hair. It's what I always do when I'm getting a brilliant idea.

"Have you still got that cactus?" I asked.

"Of course," said Ellie.

"Bingo!" I cried.

There's a back alley that runs behind the houses on Odd Street. Everybody has a gate from the alley into their yard so you can put garbage cans out and put your bike away and so on. Ivy's gate is never locked, because strangers wouldn't dare go in her yard. As soon as they saw the creepy bits of dolls sticking out of the window box, they'd turn around and run a mile—ha ha!

I explained my plan.

"Ellie, all you have to do is take your cactus out through your back gate, sneak into Ivy's yard, and swap them. Then we can take Ivy's cactus somewhere safe and a look inside the pot."

"Me?" Ellie gasped. "But what if Ivy or her mom sees me? They might think I'm a burglar, and I might go to prison. Then I'd miss school, and Mrs. Twelvetrees would send my mom a note, and if Mom got a note she'd be really upset!"

Poor Ellie. She's not really the best person to

send on dangerous missions, because she's so scared of everything. It's too bad, because she's probably the smartest of all of us and she never lets us down.

"You'll be fine," I assured her. "Me and Martha will make sure they're both at the front door, so they won't see you."

"Promise?"

"Absolutely promise," I said.

I got our spare front door key out of the kitchen drawer and showed it to the others.

"This is all we need," I said. "Come on!"

A few minutes later, I was at Ivy's front door and Martha was outside Ellie's house. I put the key on the ground, then rang Ivy's bell. When she opened the door she still had her old black top hat on.

"*Dong, dong, dong,*" said Ivy, making the bell noise. "I'm very busy! *Dong.*"

"But it's important," I said, and I pointed at the key. "Is that yours?"

Ivy came out to have a look. "I don't know," she said.

"Only one way to find out," I said, and I pulled the door shut.

"You just locked me out!" said Ivy.

"It's so we can test the key," I said.

So we tested it and it didn't work. (Surprise surprise!)

"Sorry," I said. "Never mind. You'd better ring the bell and get your mom to open the door."

Ivy reached for the bell and I winked at Martha, then Martha gave a thumbs-up to Ellie's window.

Ellie was waiting inside, and it was the signal for her to get going! By the time Ivy's mom had come to let Ivy back in, Ellie would have done the swap. Easy.

But then Ivy didn't ring the bell. "I just remembered, Mom's about to take a bath," said Ivy.

Oh, no! Ivy's bathroom window looked out over the yard just like ours did. If Ivy's mom happened to look out at the wrong time . . . eeek! Panic panic.

"Quick!" I said. "Ring the bell before she gets in the tub."

"I better not," said Ivy. "I'll just go around to the alley and get in the back way."

"NO!" I said. "No, you can't! Just ring the bell."

"Don't worry," said Ivy, about to run off. "It'll only take me a second."

What could I do? Ellie was already on her way— we had to save her!

Luckily Martha had the answer. She had heard everything, and just walked up to Ivy's front door and pushed the bell and kept her finger on it.

BURRRINGGGGGGGGGG!

"Stop it, stop it!" said Ivy. "Mom'll blow her top!"

Ivy tried to pull Martha away, but Martha is too big and strong.

"Sorry, Ivy," said Martha. "It's Agatha's idea."

What could I say? Martha was right, but Ivy didn't need to know that.

Ivy just stood there fuming while Martha kept her finger on the bell. Eventually we heard some muttering from inside.

"Time to go," said Martha, and then quick as a flash she dashed away. Gosh, it's amazing how fast she can move.

The door opened, and Ivy's mom was there wrapped in a big towel, looking very cross. There were bubbles all over her toes.

"Ivy Malting. Why did you drag your poor mother out of the bath?"

"Agatha locked me out!" said Ivy.

"I've a good mind to lock you out myself," said Ivy's mom. "Now come in and take that hat off. It's giving me the creeps."

The doorbell thing was all kind of embarrassing, but soon Martha and Ellie and me had regrouped in my yard with Ivy's cactus. I thought cactuses were supposed to be green, but this one was more like gray, and it looked kind of dead.

When we tipped it out, we saw a little lumpy white paper bag rolled up in the bottom.

"It looks very small," said Ellie.

"Random was only a baby," I said, and we were all nearly crying.

"Do you think chickens have ghosts?" asked Ellie, which made us laugh as well as cry at the same time. It was bit like *boo hoo HA HA boo hoo HA HA*, and that gives you a really runny nose.

Martha picked the bag up with the very ends of her fingertips in case she got ghost chicken germs. It didn't look quite right. To start with, the bag was soaking wet, and the lump we could see through the paper was more orange than yellow. Martha unrolled it and we looked inside.

It was a fish!

"That's Gilbert," said Ellie. "Ivy said he was unwell, and now he's dead."

No wonder Ivy's mom had been so upset when she had come over to our house. She'd had Gilbert for years. She used to teach him tricks and everything.

Suddenly a loud shriek came over the wall from Ivy's yard.

"WOW oh WOW oh WOW!" we heard Ivy screaming. "WOWWWW!"

We charged in the back door and up the stairs, past Dad on the wobbly ladder—

"DO YOU MIND???" shouted Dad.

"Sorry, Dad!"

—and then into the bathroom, climbed on the tub, and looked out the window.

Ivy was staring at the cactus.

"She's noticed that it's different," said Martha.

"But I thought they were exactly the same," I said.

"They used to be," said Ellie. "But there was something I forgot to tell you . . ."

But before Ellie could finish, Ivy picked up the cactus and turned it around.

"Wow!" said me and Martha.

"That's what I forgot to tell you," said Ellie. "Our cactus grew a pink flower."

"Hey, Mom!" shouted Ivy, staring at the flower. "Our cactus is MAGIC!"

Martha and me started to giggle, but Ellie climbed down off the tub and gave us a cross look.

"Stop it, you two," said Ellie. "That's not fair. I wouldn't have changed the cactus if I'd known you were going to make fun of Ivy."

"We're not making fun of anyone," I said. "We love Ivy."

"We're just giggling," said Martha.

"But it's not funny," said Ellie.

Ivy must have heard us because suddenly she looked up at our bathroom window. Me and Martha quickly stepped out of sight, and guess what? We'd forgotten to shut the toilet lid, so we both ended up with one foot in the toilet.

"YARGH!" we went.

"Ha ha ha!" Ellie laughed. "Now that IS funny!"

The Lump of Doom

That night, everybody was asleep except for me, and it was all Tilly's fault.

If she hadn't opened the shoebox and let the chickens out, then I'd have known for sure if there had been three or four. As it was, I was lying awake on the top bunk, worrying myself sick about Random while she was nicely asleep on the bottom bunk, making funny little *moo* sounds into her pillow. Rotten kid.

The shoebox was on the chair with the three chicks snuggled up inside it, making little chicken snorey noises. All I could do was lie there and listen for anything that might be Random walking around the house.

It was exactly 2:31 a.m. on my alarm clock when I heard a very quiet little tapping noise. It was coming from the staircase landing.

I rushed out and turned the light on. The sound stopped, and there was nothing moving. Dad had been working really late finishing the wallpaper, and the towels were still all over the place. I went down the stairs, picking them up and looking around,

but there was no sign of
Random. When I got to
the bottom, I heard the
tapping again. It was a
bug flying around in the
lampshade. Boring!

I started back upstairs.
Mom wasn't going to be
too happy with the wallpaper! It was all crooked
with lots of sticky patches, and there was a weird
lump under the paper by the top step. It was about
the size of a sausage, or perhaps a potato . . . or an
egg . . . or a *baby chicken!*

PANIC PANIC!

It was obvious what must have happened. When

Dad was waving his wet paper around, Random had gotten stuck to it, and now he was glued to the wall!

I stared at the lump to see if it was moving. It wasn't. I put my ear to it and listened. No sound.

"Random, are you in there?" I whispered.

The lump didn't answer. Then I remembered how Miss Bunn had gotten the chickens to respond to her when they were still in their eggs. I clicked my tongue a little then started to sing:

"Chick chick chick chick

CHICKEN!

Lay a little egg for me.

Chick chick chick chick

CHICKEN!

Lay one, lay two, lay three!"

As I was singing, I started picking at the edge of the wallpaper to see if I could peel it back.

"What are you doing?" asked James.

Oh, rats! I looked up and saw James watching me over the banister.

"I was just getting a drink of water," I said.

"Liar," said James. "Your singing woke me up. And why are you trying to pull the wallpaper off?"

"Don't be silly," I said. "You're having a dream."

All I could do was get back into bed and hope that James would forget all about it.

I plunked my head on the pillow and shut my eyes, but then I heard a scratching sound outside the door. I wasn't going to get up, in case James was still around, but the scratching got louder and louder. Suddenly there was a giant ripping noise, and then I heard creaky footsteps coming into the bedroom.

"Ag—ath—aaa!" a screechy voice called out. "Agathaaa, why didn't you save meee?"

"Who are you?" I said, only I didn't say it, because when I talked I could only make chicken noises. *"Eeeep peep zik!"*

"I am Ran-DOOOOM, the chicken ghost! Why didn't you save meee?"

EEEKY FREAK! I rolled up into a tiny ball under my covers.

"It wasn't my fault!" I said, but it came out like *"Deek eeep wee!"*

I knew something very big was looking over the edge of the top bunk.

"Answer me or I will peck through your tights."

Eh? I wasn't wearing tights. I was in bed. But then I felt my legs. Oh, no, I WAS wearing tights! It was my horrible old woolly tights too. How did they get there?

"I will peck through your tights and your LEG WILL FALL OFF . . . leg will fall off . . . leg will fall off . . ."

And then I woke up.

Bah! I felt like such a dolt. I'd been having Ellie's dream about chickens. I sat up and pulled my hair to get my brain working. There was no giant chicken, I wasn't wearing tights, and it was morning—I could tell because I could hear voices out on the landing.

"It looks awful," said Mom. "We'll have to save up to hire a real decorator."

"If that's what you want," said Dad. "Or we could leave it and save up for concert tickets instead?"

"Concert tickets? Really?" said Mom, sounding excited. "Okay, you've got a deal, but only if you get rid of that big lump."

A big lump? So the lump wasn't part of the dream. Maybe Random was in there after all?

By the time I was dressed, the others were down in the kitchen still having the wallpaper conversation.

"You could try squashing that lump with your foot," said Mom.

"NO!" I said a bit too loudly.

"Agatha's right," said Dad. "It might make a nasty mess."

EEEK! If that lump was what I thought it was,

then it would be a lot nastier than Dad was expecting!

"What do you think the lump is?" asked Mom.

I was glad she was asking Dad and not me.

"A big blob of wet glue," said Dad. "I could stick a pin in it, then squeeze it so all the glue comes out."

"NO, NO, YOU CAN'T!" I screamed.

"Are you all right?" Dad asked.

"Ignore her," said James, who was eating his cornflakes. "She was singing about chickens to that lump last night. She's gone 'round the bend."

"I have NOT gone 'round the bend," I said.

And that's when Dad looked out of the kitchen door and said: "Speaking of chickens, there's a giant chicken coming down the stairs."

ARGHHH!

I was about to dive under the table, when I suddenly realized—

"This is another dream, isn't it?" I said. "I'm not awake at all. There's no giant chicken."

"Yes, there is," said Dad.

"He's right, there is," said Mom, who had gone to look.

"No there ISN'T!" I said. "I *know* it's a dream. None of this is real!"

And just to show it was a dream and nothing really mattered and we'd all wake up, I got on the table, picked up the cornflake box, and tipped it out all over my head.

"See?" I said. "I wouldn't be doing this if it was real, would I?"

Mom and Dad looked at me like I was an alien. Then Tilly came in through the door wearing her paper chicken head and some yellow tights and a yellow T-shirt and a set of fairy wings.

"What's Agatha doing?" asked Tilly.

"Agatha thought you were a real chicken." James laughed.

"Tilly's dressed up for the school chicken assembly," explained Mom. "It's a very good costume, Tilly!"

"It certainly fooled Agatha," said Dad.

Don't Count Your Chickens Before They Hatch!

On the way to school, I met up with the others. We had four shoeboxes with three chickens each.

"Three times four makes twelve," said Ellie, who's our numbers expert.

"Can't it make thirteen sometimes?" asked Martha hopefully.

"Never!" said Ellie strictly.

It was all right for Ellie. She was the only one of us who KNEW she hadn't lost a chicken. The rest of us were worried sick.

Motley was waiting for us by the school entrance.

"Mrs. Twelvetrees wants me to put the chickens in the brooding box so they're ready for the assembly," he said, holding his hands out.

All we could do was hand the boxes over and hope that nobody else remembered how many chickens there were supposed to be.

By the time we'd put our coats and bags away, we were the last people to arrive at the assembly. There was a great big sheet of cardboard in the middle of the floor, and all the kiddies were sitting around it wearing their chicken hats and any other costumes they had. The place was full of cowboy chickens, fairy chickens, alien chickens—and one little kiddie had put on his Halloween outfit and come as a chicken-headed pumpkin. EEEEK!

Everybody else had to stand behind the kiddies. Me and Martha and Ivy and Bianca stayed close to the door in case we needed to make a quick escape. If the kiddies realized there was a chicken missing, it could get nasty. None of us wanted to face an angry pumpkin-headed chicken.

Mrs. Twelvetrees was standing next to Motley's brooding box, and right beside her was Miss Barking

looking very serious. Miss B. had her mask and big gloves on, and she was holding a little fishing net on the end of a stick. Thank goodness! We could all relax knowing that if a chicken decided to go crazy and attack our beloved principal, then Miss Barking would dive in and save her. YAY! Give that woman a medal.

Mrs. Twelvetrees clapped her hands, and we all got quiet.

"What a thrilling day!" Mrs. Twelvetrees said. "We're here to welcome our new visitors, the chickens!"

"HOORAY!" cheered everybody.

"Miss Bunn's class gave all the chickens special names," said Mrs. T. "Who can remember them all?"

Over by the door we breathed a big sigh of relief. *PHEW!* We didn't know what names the little kiddies had given the chickens, but there was no way they would remember thirteen different names, so nobody would realize there was one missing.

Flozzie Slippin put her hand up. "I can remember the names," she said.

"What are they?" asked Mrs. Twelvetrees.

"One, Two, Three, Four, Five, Six, Seven, Eight, Nine, Ten, Eleven, Twelve, and Thirteen!"

"That's right, Flozzie," said Mrs. T. "The chickens are named after numbers!"

Oh, no! That was NOT what we wanted to hear.

"So how many chickens should we have in here?" asked Mrs. Twelvetrees, tapping the brooding box. She was really rubbing it in.

"Thirteen!" cheered all the kiddies.

"And who can count to thirteen?" asked Mrs. T.

"We can!" The kiddies cheered again.

We all felt really awful, and then Mrs. T. made it even worse.

"Before we count the chickens, let's have a big round of applause for our chicken monitors, who looked after them last night. Well done, Ivy, Martha, Agatha, and Bianca. Where are you, girls?"

Mrs. Twelvetrees was peering around the hall. We sneaked toward the door, but Miss Pingle got in the way.

"Here they are!" called out Miss Pingle helpfully.

"HURRAH!" cheered all the kiddies, and everybody gave us a big round of applause.

Normally I like getting applause, but all I could think about was the lump in the wallpaper. I felt totally rotten. It would have served me right if Ran-Doom the chicken ghost had pecked through my woolly tights after all.

"Let's have the first chicken, Miss Barking," said Mrs. Twelvetrees. "Everybody get ready to count!"

Miss Barking went up to the

box and reached in, but then she stopped and made a puzzled face.

"She's noticed!" gasped Martha. "Stand by for big trouble."

"Come on, Miss Barking," said Mrs. Twelvetrees. "Everyone's waiting!"

Miss Barking got a chicken out and carefully put it on the cardboard.

"One!" counted the kiddies.

"He's lovely!" said Mrs. Twelvetrees.

"That's not Lovely, that's Drain Pump," whispered Ivy.

Miss Barking kept going.

"Two, three, four . . ." counted the kiddies as the chickens arrived and huddled together on the cardboard.

"Five, six, seven, eight, nine . . ."

"Isn't this FUN?" said Mrs. T.

"Ten, eleven . . ." chanted the kiddies.

But then Miss Barking stopped. She was staring in the box again.

"Come on, Miss Barking," Mrs. T said again. "We want to see all thirteen chickens, then put them back before they get cold."

"Oh, dear," said Miss Barking, and then she pulled out the twelfth chicken.

"Twelve!" cheered the kiddies.

Everybody was waiting for the thirteenth chicken.

Miss Barking obviously didn't know what to do. She was still staring into the box.

"Something's gone wrong," said Miss Barking.

"Oh!" said all the kiddies. Everybody sounded really worried.

"They are so going to hate us," I said.

"I don't blame them," said Martha sadly.

Miss Barking started fiddling with the red light over Motley's box and prodded the control.

"I said it wasn't safe," she said. "But they never listen."

Mrs. Twelvetrees went to take a look.

"What is it?" she asked, then looked into the box. "GOOD GOLLY!"

Very carefully she reached her hands in and pulled out . . . a purple chicken!

"THIRTEEN!" shouted the kiddies.

"Thirteen?" we gasped.

Mrs. T. put the purple chicken on the floor, and it wasn't any old purple chicken, either! He toddled straight over to where Gwendoline was standing and left a great big POOP!

WAHOO!

There was only one little fluffy person it could be . . . RANDOM!

Who Did It and How?

The rest of Friday was a complete blur. We must have had lessons and lunchtime and everything, but I couldn't concentrate. All I could think about was the big mystery. How did Random come to be purple?

At the very end of the day, we had a math quiz, and Miss Pingle handed out the sheets for us to fill in. Everybody else started writing, but I was too busy looking around the class for clues. Some purple chicken footprints next to a big pot of purple paint would have been helpful, but I couldn't see anything like that. All I could see was Liam quietly slipping an old apple core into Matt's reading bag—ha ha! Actually, you shouldn't laugh at boys—it only encourages them.

I started to doodle on the corner of the quiz. Big mistake! The next thing I knew, everybody was getting ready to go home, and Ivy was shaking my shoulder.

"Come on, Agatha!" she said. "Haven't you finished?"

I looked down at my

sheet. I'd drawn a fabulous chicken with thirty wings and beaks and teeth and a flower growing out of its tail.

"Very nice!" Ivy laughed. "But you better write some answers in quickly. We'll wait for you out by the gate."

Soon it was just me and Miss Pingle left in the classroom. I was desperately trying to fill the sheet in while she was packing up her bag.

"Time to go, Agatha!" she said. "It's the weekend. I've got plans, and I'm afraid they don't include you."

She came to get the quiz from me, but as soon as she walked away from her bag, it fell over. Everything slid out onto the floor.

"Oh, no!" she said. "It always does that."

She stood the bag up, but before she could put anything back in, it fell over again.

"Why don't you get another bag?" I asked.

"I should," she admitted. "But I just love the color too much."

The color?

I found myself staring at the bag and then at Miss Pingle's hair. I was getting a crazy idea, and I was probably making a crazy face to go with it.

"Agatha?" said Miss Pingle. "Hello? Are you all right?"

"Fine!" I said. "I just wanted to ask you something. Did you notice anything unusual about the thirteenth chicken today?"

"Er . . . why?" asked Miss Pingle. She sounded

a little nervous, and she had every reason to be!

"What color would you say that chicken was?"

"A sort of purple," said Miss P.

"Oh, really?" I said. "Because if you ask me, I'd say it was more like . . . *Damson Dream!*"

Miss Pingle stared down at her bag and patted her hair at the same time.

"Did you dye him to match your hair?" I asked.

"NO!" exclaimed Miss P.

She tried not to look at me, but I was giving her a HARD STARE. It was like slowly squishing a banana. There was nothing Miss Pingle could do to resist my awesome eyeball power!

"Well, I didn't do it on purpose," she said. "Honest!"

"Let me guess," I said. "When the chickens were running around yesterday, your bag fell over, and he snuck in."

"He must have," said Miss Pingle. "Then when I got home, my bag fell over again. He hopped out and ran to hide behind my trash can."

"And he found some of your hair dye."

Miss Pingle nodded. "There was a tissue on the floor with a big blob on it, and he got tangled up in it. I tried to wash the dye off with a bit of warm water, but he turned purple!"

Poor Miss P. The only thing she could do after that was sneak him back into school and slip him into the brooding box before the assembly.

"I felt bad, but he seemed happy enough. I'm

just glad that none of you spent last night worrying about where he was," said Miss P.

"Oh, no, of course not," I said.

Well, I was hardly going to say I thought Random was a giant chicken ghost that had come out of a lump in our wallpaper and made me tip cornflakes all over my head, was I?

The Odd Street Miracle

That's the end of the main story, but there is one more thing to tell you, because it's my favorite part!

It happened just after I'd seen Miss Pingle. I met all the others out on the playground, and we walked slowly up Odd Street to our houses. They had a good laugh when I told them what had happened to Random.

"Will he be purple forever?" asked Ellie.

"Only until his guff flows," said Bianca.

"Until his *guff flows?*" said everybody.

"His guff flows, and then he fets his gethers," said Bianca.

It took me a minute before I got it.

"His *fluff goes,* and then he *gets* his *feathers!*" I said.

By the time we'd figured out what Bianca was saying, we were standing outside number 1, where she lives.

"Bye-bye, Bianca," I said. "Sorry I blamed you for blowing a chicken out of your trombone!"

"That's okay," said Bianca. "You were right to check it out, even if you were wrong."

"So Agatha was right and wrong at the same time?" asked Ivy. "That's a neat trick!"

We waved at Bianca, and in she went.

Next was Martha's house at number 3.

"Sorry I blamed you for making Random explode," I said.

"Forget it," said Martha. "We know Random's your favorite, and at least he came back safe and sound. Overall, I'd say we did a pretty good job. YO!" Then she high-fived us all and went in too.

When we got to number 5 where I live, there was just Ivy and Ellie left.

"I'm *really* sorry about your cactus, Ivy," I said.

"Our cactus?" asked Ivy. "What's our cactus got to do with anything?"

Oops!

I shouldn't have said anything, because Ellie got into a real panic.

"It's got nothing to do with anything," said Ellie. "Nothing. NOTHING."

Ellie ran off into her house at number 9.

Ivy gave me a suspicious look.

"What's been going on?" she asked.

But before I could think of what to say, Ivy's front door opened.

"Bless you, Maria!" said a big booming voice from inside. "I'm so glad you asked me to come."

"That sounds like Father Bartles," said Ivy. "He's the priest from our church."

A very big man in black clothes stepped out, followed by Ivy's mom. He scratched his chin thoughtfully.

"Are you sure that cactus was dead yesterday morning?" he asked.

"Dead as a doornail," said Ivy's mom. "And so that little flower must be a present from my dear Gilbert up in heaven! Mustn't it?"

"Why not?" Father Bartles laughed. "I'll write it up in my parish report. I shall call it the Odd Street Miracle!"

Ivy's mom did a little happy hoppy skip dance, just like Ivy does, and she had the BIGGEST smile on her face.

Father Bartles got on his bike, and then, with a bit of a wobble, pedaled off down the road. "See you on Sunday!" he shouted.

Ivy's mom kept on waving after him, even

after he'd disappeared around the corner. Then she did another little happy hoppy skip dance and went inside.

Ivy grabbed me and gave me a big hug.

"Thanks for cheering her up," she said.

"Me?" I said. "What did I do?"

SQUEAK
SQUEAK

"I don't know," admitted Ivy. "But the cactus, the flower, Mom being happy again . . . it HAS to have something to do with you!"

I was just about to tell her, but she covered up her ears.

"Oh, no, don't tell me!" said Ivy. "Then it wouldn't be a miracle anymore!"

Then she ran inside shouting, "MIRACLE MIRACLE MIRACLE!" and slammed her door with a great big WHAM.

So it's official. It was a miracle, and everybody on Odd Street lived happily ever after!

Even the cactus had a good time, because Ivy kept putting little bits of fish food in the pot in case Gilbert's ghost was feeling hungry. And that's not a joke, because we all believe in ghosts on Odd Street because our school had one!

I'm not kidding. It was a horrible figure that glowed in the dark, and we ALL saw it through the windows. EEEKY FREAK! It all started when . . . Oh, sorry!

I'll have to tell you about the ghost another time, because the old man who's typing this book out says we've only got a few pages left, and I've got a puzzle for you to try! I wasn't going to tell you the answer, but the old man said that was unfair, so here's a little secret—the answer is on page 69, 14 lines down, and it's the last word, but DON'T LOOK YET!

Before you put this book away, if you've read it

all by yourself, then you deserve a big treat.
Bend your mouth around and give yourself
a big KISS on the cheek. Ha ha, don't
worry! I'm only kidding so don't bother—
unless you want to, of course.

See you next time, and good luck with
the puzzle!

BYEEEEEEE . . .

The Chicken Puzzle
by Agatha Jane Parrot

There were four eggs in Miss Bunn's class, painted blue, pink, green, and yellow. Four chickens, called Wizzy, Tubby, Drain Pump, and Random, hatched out of the eggs. Here are some clues:

- The green egg was the second to hatch.
- Drain Pump was the third chicken to hatch, but he did not come out of the pink egg.

- When Tubby hatched, the blue egg still hadn't opened.
- Wizzy came out of the yellow egg, and he wasn't the last.

Here's the question . . .

What color was Random's egg?

Psst! If you need a hint, follow this line . . . ➡

(Hint: Work out what color Drain Pump's egg was. Then what color egg was last to hatch. Then which chicken was last to hatch.)

Hey!

Do you want to know more about me and my friends?

Or how about trying my book quiz?

Or maybe you'd like to see some fun facts?

Check out my website: www.agathaparrot.com.

You can also find out about my other books, and there are some games you can print out and play— WAHOO!

Hope to see you soon!

Agatha xoxo